Here's what kids and grown-ups have to say about the Magic Tree House® books:

"Oh, man . . . the Magic Tree House series
is really exciting!"
—Christina

"I like the Magic Tree House series. I stay up
all night reading them. Even on school nights!"
—Peter

"Jack and Annie have opened a door to a world
of literacy that I know will continue throughout
the lives of my students."
—Deborah H.

"As a librarian, I have seen many happy young
readers coming into the library to check out
the next Magic Tree House book in the series."
—Lynne H.

Magic Tree House®

For a list of Magic Tree House® Merlin Missions and other
Magic Tree House titles, visit MagicTreeHouse.com.

MAGIC TREE HOUSE®

#30 HURRICANE HEROES IN TEXAS

BY MARY POPE OSBORNE

ILLUSTRATIONS BY AG FORD

A STEPPING STONE BOOK™

Random House 🏠 New York

To all volunteers and first responders who
rush forward to help others

Text copyright © 2018 by Mary Pope Osborne
Cover art and interior illustrations copyright © 2018 by AG Ford

Visit us on the Web!
rhcbooks.com
MagicTreeHouse.com

Educators and librarians, for a variety of teaching tools, visit us at
RHTeachersLibrarians.com

The Library of Congress has cataloged the hardcover edition of this work as follows:
Names: Osborne, Mary Pope, author. | Ford, AG, illustrator.
Title: Hurricane heroes in Texas / by Mary Pope Osborne ; illustrated by AG Ford.
Description: New York : Random House, [2018] | Series: Magic tree house ; #30 |
Summary: "Jack and Annie travel in the magic tree house to Galveston, Texas, on September 8, 1900—the day of the worst natural disaster in US history" —Provided by publisher.
Identifiers: LCCN 2017049749 | ISBN 978-1-5247-1312-6 (trade) |
ISBN 978-1-5247-1313-3 (lib. bdg.) | ISBN 978-1-5247-1314-0 (ebook)
Subjects: | CYAC: Time travel—Fiction. | Hurricanes—Texas—Galveston—History—20th century—Fiction. | Magic—Fiction. | Tree houses—Fiction. | Galveston (Tex.)—History—20th century—Fiction.
Classification: LCC PZ7.O81167 Hum 2018 | DDC [Fic]—dc23

ISBN 978-1-5247-1315-7 (pbk.)

Printed in the United States of America

10 9 8 7 6 5

This book has been officially leveled by using the F&P Text Level Gradient™ Leveling System.

CONTENTS

Dear Reader,

In the summer of 2017, I began writing a book about the most devastating hurricane in the history of the United States. It happened in Galveston, Texas, in 1900. As I wrote about the monster hurricane, Texas was hit by another dangerous storm: Hurricane Harvey. Like Galveston more than a hundred years before, the people of Texas were slammed with powerful winds, record rainfall, and life-threatening floods. I could hardly believe it was all happening again—and just when I was writing this book! Both events were terrible disasters, but it is from tragedy that heroes rise. This book is inspired by the hope and courage of Texans.

Mary Pope Osborne

PROLOGUE

One summer day in Frog Creek, Pennsylvania, a mysterious tree house appeared in the woods. It was filled with books. A boy named Jack and his sister, Annie, found the tree house and soon discovered that it was magic. They could go to any time and place in history just by pointing to a picture in one of the books. While they were gone, no time at all passed back in Frog Creek.

Jack and Annie eventually found out that the tree house belonged to Morgan le Fay, a magical librarian from the legendary realm of Camelot.

1

Since then, they have traveled on many adventures in the magic tree house and completed many missions for Morgan.

In Magic Tree House books #29–32, Morgan has given Jack and Annie a new challenge: they must learn important truths from heroes who have helped the world.

On their last adventure, Jack and Annie learned a great lesson from baseball star Jackie Robinson. Now they are about to find out where Morgan will send them next. . . .

1

LONE STAR STATE

Jack and Annie sat on their front porch. They were waiting for their mom to take them to baseball practice.

Tap, tap, tap.

Raindrops spattered on the porch steps. A strong breeze shook the tree leaves.

"Uh-oh," said Annie. "Do you think a storm is coming?"

"I can't tell," said Jack, looking up at the clouds.

"Sorry, kids," their mom called from inside. "Coach Dave just emailed—no practice today."

"Darn," said Jack.

"That's okay," said Annie. "Now we can go to the woods."

"The woods?" said Jack. "Why?"

"I woke up with a feeling," Annie said in a hushed voice. "Something really important is going to happen today. I thought it was baseball practice, like maybe I'd hit a home run or something. But now . . ." She smiled at Jack.

"Really? You think . . . ?" he said.

"Yes! Hold on! I'll get our stuff." Annie hurried inside.

A moment later, she returned with two small umbrellas and Jack's backpack. She handed over the pack and one of the umbrellas. "Mom says as long as there's no thunder and lightning, we can take a walk."

"Great," said Jack. He pulled on his pack. "To the woods!"

"To the tree house!" said Annie.

Jack and Annie opened their umbrellas and headed out into the rain. They ran down the sidewalk, across the street, and into the misty Frog Creek woods.

Raindrops fell softly as they hurried between the trees. The air smelled of wet leaves and damp earth.

Finally, Jack and Annie came to the tallest oak in the woods.

"Yay," Jack whispered.

Annie laughed. "Glad it rained today?"

"Totally," said Jack. He and Annie folded their umbrellas and climbed up the rope ladder.

The magic tree house was dry and shadowy inside. A book was lying on the floor. A purple leather bookmark was sticking out from between the pages.

Lying on top of the book was a necklace. It had a thin gold chain and a glass star. The star was no bigger than a penny. It gave off a soft yellow glow.

"Wow, a little star!" said Annie, picking up the necklace. "I wonder what it's for."

"Yeah, and where are we going?" asked Jack. He picked up the book.

The cover showed a red, white, and blue flag with one big star. The title said:

A History of Texas:
The Lone Star State

"Great. Back to Texas!" said Jack.

"I love Texas," said Annie. "Remember when we met Slim and saved Dusty's colt?"

"Yup," Jack said in a low voice. Annie laughed. Jack was imitating their cowboy friend, Slim.

Jack turned to the page with the purple bookmark. He and Annie looked at an old black-and-white photo of a city by the ocean.

"*Galveston, Texas,*" read Annie. "I've heard of that city."

"Me too," said Jack. "Did Morgan leave us a note?"

"I don't see one," said Annie. "Is anything written on the back of the bookmark?"

Jack turned the bookmark over. "Yes!" he said. Tiny writing was painted on the leather. He read aloud:

The place you must go
On this late summer day
Is an island in Texas
Between Gulf and bay.

"We're here to help!"
Is what you must say.
"Seek high ground now!
Do not delay!"

Jack looked up. "Why do people need help?" he asked. "And why should they seek high ground?"

"Good questions," said Annie. "Keep reading."

Jack read the next part:

For those in the dark,
Adrift and astray,
A single bright star
Can show them the way.

"So that must explain *this,*" said Annie. She held up the necklace with the star.

"But it's so small," said Jack. "And it's not really bright. How can it show the way to anything?"

"Go on, read the last part," said Annie.

Jack read the last lines of the rhyme:

Learn from a hero
Who is humble and brave,

Who welcomes the hundreds
Arriving on waves.

"What does *that* mean?" asked Jack.

"I don't know," said Annie. "Let's go to Texas and find out all the answers." She hung the star necklace around her neck.

"Wait—do we have our Pennsylvania book to help us get back home?" said Jack. They looked around the tree house.

"There—" said Annie. She pointed to the Pennsylvania book, in a shadowy corner.

"Okay, all set," said Jack. He placed his finger on the picture of Galveston, Texas.

"I wish we could go *there!*" he said.

The wind started to blow.

The tree house started to spin.

It spun faster and faster.

Then everything was still.

Absolutely still.

9

2

WELCOME TO GALVESTON!

Tap, tap, tap.

Soft rain fell on the roof of the tree house. A gentle breeze shook the tree leaves outside.

"Old-fashioned clothes," said Annie.

She and Jack were both wearing stockings, leather shoes, and shirts with sailor collars. Annie wore a cotton skirt, and Jack wore knee pants. Their two small umbrellas had changed into one large black umbrella with a bamboo handle. Jack's backpack was now a thick canvas knapsack.

"We wore clothes like these when we went to

San Francisco in 1906," said Jack. "Maybe we've come to the same time."

He and Annie looked out the window.

The tree house had landed in a spreading oak

tree in someone's backyard. From the window, Jack and Annie could see all the way across the city of Galveston. They saw wooden houses, fancy-looking mansions, stables and barns, horse buggies, and street trolleys.

"This could definitely be the early 1900s," said Annie. "No cars or trucks anywhere."

"Right," said Jack. He pulled out their Texas book and found *Galveston* in the index. He read aloud:

The city of Galveston, Texas, was built on a long, narrow island between the Gulf of Mexico and Galveston Bay.

"Exactly what our rhyme says—*an island in Texas between Gulf and bay*," said Annie.

Jack kept reading:

In the late 1800s, Galveston was the third busiest

12

seaport in the United States. Ships from all over the world docked there. The thriving city had almost 40,000 residents. It was also a popular tourist resort.

"That's us—a couple of tourists," said Annie. "Come on. Let's explore the city."

"Okay," said Jack. "But the main thing we have to do is find the people Morgan wants us to help."

Jack put their Texas book in his knapsack. Annie grabbed their old-fashioned umbrella.

"Wow, this is heavy!" she said.

"Toss it to the ground," Jack said.

Annie lowered the long folded umbrella out the window and dropped it. Then she and Jack climbed down the rope ladder. As they stepped onto the soggy grass, the rain fell harder.

Jack picked up the umbrella and opened it. It *was* heavy! And awkward! But its black canopy easily covered both of them.

"Hey, people are home in that house," said Annie. "Hear them?"

Not far from the oak tree was a blue house with a wide front porch. It was set about five feet off the ground on brick pillars.

From an open window came the cries of a baby, and then a woman's voice singing:

Hush, little baby, don't say a word.
Papa's going to buy you a mockingbird. . . .

"She has a pretty voice," said Annie.

"Yeah, but let's hurry out of her yard before she discovers us—and the tree house," said Jack.

Holding the huge umbrella over them, Jack walked with Annie to the gate of an iron fence. Then they slipped out of the yard onto a street.

"Look, we're on Avenue L," said Jack, pointing to a street sign. "When it's time to get back to the tree house, we'll need to come back here."

"Got it," said Annie. "Blue house, iron fence, Avenue L."

Rain pelted their umbrella as Jack and Annie started down the avenue. The street was lined with spreading oaks and wooden houses. Nearly all the houses had wide front porches and were set on brick pillars. Small children were playing in rain puddles.

A gust of wind nearly ripped the umbrella out of Jack's hands. The wind blew the rain sideways,

soaking their clothes. A horse and buggy clattered past, and mud spattered their shoes and stockings.

"Yikes, let's get inside somewhere," said Annie.

"Good idea," said Jack.

Jack and Annie walked faster, until they turned the corner of Avenue L and 25th Street. Heading down 25th, they passed a blacksmith shop, a shoemaker, and a hatmaker.

Annie stopped in front of the Lone Star Café.

"Should we go in there?" she asked.

"Yes!" said Jack, and he closed their huge umbrella.

A bell jangled over the door as Jack and Annie entered the crowded café. The warm, damp room smelled of coffee and bacon.

Jack and Annie sat at a table near a rain-streaked window. They watched others hurry into the café—men in cowboy hats and suits and women in flowered bonnets and long skirts. Everyone seemed cheerful as they shook the rain from their umbrellas and hats.

"So who exactly are we supposed to help in Galveston?" said Jack. "And where's 'high ground'?"

"I'll ask," said Annie. She turned to a gray-haired couple at the table next to them. "Excuse me, where is 'high ground' in Galveston?"

"'High ground' is that way, missy," said the elderly man, pointing to the right. "We call it 'uptown.'"

"The lowest ground is along the Strand," said the woman in a squeaky voice. She pointed to the left. "It's the street that runs beside the Gulf. But that's a funny question. You're not from here, are you?"

"No, we're tourists from Pennsylvania," said Annie.

"Well, welcome to Galveston!" said the woman.

"Thanks!" said Annie. She turned back to Jack. "One question answered."

17

"Good, but we have more," he said. He pulled out their Texas book and read softly to Annie:

By the end of the 1800s, many considered the island city of Galveston to be the leading city in Texas. Its port was filled with ships. Its hotels and restaurants were filled with tourists. Its neighborhoods had nice homes and schools. The city seemed to have everything.

"Sounds like a great place," said Annie. Jack kept reading:

But one day, all that changed.

"Uh-oh," said Annie. Jack read on:

On September 8, 1900, Galveston suffered the worst natural disaster in U.S. history. A deadly storm, later known as the Great Galveston Hurricane, swept across the island.

"Oh, man," said Jack. A scary thought came to him. His heart started to pound. "What's today's date?" he asked.

Annie turned back to the couple. "Excuse me again, do you know today's date?" she asked.

"September eighth," the woman said with a friendly smile.

"Nineteen-hundred?" Jack asked.

"Why, yes. You didn't know that?" the woman asked.

Jack just shrugged. His mouth was suddenly so dry, he could hardly speak. He looked back at Annie. Her eyes were huge.

"We got here just in time," Annie whispered.

"Right," said Jack. *For the worst natural disaster in U.S. history.*

3

SEEK HIGH GROUND!

"It doesn't *look* like a day for a huge disaster," said Annie.

Outside the café, people were clinging to their windblown umbrellas. But no one looked scared. Some even laughed as a man chased his cowboy hat down the sidewalk.

At the café counter, a policeman was eating a sandwich and joking with a waitress. He didn't seem worried. *No one* seemed worried! Customers were cheerfully chatting with each other or reading newspapers.

"What does the newspaper say?" asked Annie.

"I'll check," said Jack. He jumped up and grabbed a copy of the *Galveston Daily News* from an empty table. He sat back down and scanned the front page. Near the bottom was a small headline:

STORM IN THE GULF

"Listen!" Jack said to Annie. He read aloud:

The awaited Gulf storm has moved north over Cuba. The weather bureau reports no new information about the storm's movements. Most likely, it changed course before reaching Texas.

Jack put down the paper. "That's so wrong," he said. "It's heading straight for Galveston."

"I don't get it," said Annie. "Why doesn't the weather bureau know that a terrible hurricane is coming?"

"I guess because in 1900, they didn't have radar or satellites," said Jack. "They didn't have computers or TV or weather apps or—"

"Okay. Got it," said Annie.

Jack picked up their book again. His heart was racing as he read aloud:

On September 8, Galveston was completely unprepared for a terrible hurricane. For eight hours, raging winds and water rushed across the island. Thousands of lives were lost in the storm surge.

"Thousands of lives? That's terrible!" said Annie. "What's a storm surge?"

"It's when high winds push the ocean water over land," Jack said. He kept reading:

Seawater from both the Gulf and the bay covered the whole island. Those who fled to higher

22

ground had a better chance of surviving. Many found safety in tall, sturdy buildings, such as the Tremont House hotel and the Ursuline Academy.

"Morgan's message makes perfect sense now," said Annie. "We have to help people. We literally have to tell them to *'seek high ground now'* and *'do not delay!'*"

She turned back to the elderly couple at the next table.

"Excuse me, but we have information that a powerful hurricane is coming here today," she said. "Everyone needs to seek high ground."

"Or go to the Tremont House," Jack said. "Or the Ursuline Academy."

The woman smiled at them. "You're both so sweet wanting to help everyone. We're expecting a bad storm, but not a hurricane," she said.

"She's right," the man said. "And we're used to bad storms here. That's why many of our houses are raised up on pillars. It keeps the floodwaters from coming in."

Jack just nodded. "Okay. Thanks," he said. He didn't know what else to do. He couldn't show them a book from the future!

"Jack, we have to tell someone in charge," Annie said. "How about that policeman? He should be the one to warn everyone."

"Okay," said Jack.

Jack put their Texas book into his knapsack.

Annie grabbed their umbrella. They hurried over to the policeman.

"Excuse me, sir," said Annie. "We have reliable information that Galveston is about to have the worst natural disaster in U.S. history."

"That's right, sir," said Jack, trying to sound calm. "Everyone needs to seek higher ground or find shelter in tall, sturdy buildings."

The jolly-looking policeman grinned. "And where did you kids get your information?" he said.

"Uh . . . someone told us," said Jack. "Someone really smart."

"Well, shame on them for scaring you," the policeman said. "I spoke to our local weatherman this morning. He said we're going to have strong winds and some bad rain, but nothing more."

"But he's wrong, sir," said Annie. "We're telling you the facts."

"I don't want you to worry, little girl," the policeman said kindly. "Why don't you go have fun with all the young folks down on the Strand? They're having a grand time watching the big waves roll in. I was just down there."

Annie whirled back to Jack. "The *Strand*!" she said. "That's the *lowest* ground!"

"Oh, no!" said Jack. "We have to warn them!"

"Thanks for the tip," Annie said to the policeman. Then she and Jack raced out into the driving rain.

Water was rushing down the sidewalk. Jack struggled to open their huge umbrella. But the wind yanked it from his hands and carried it down the block.

"Oh, no! There goes the umbrella!" said Jack.

"That's okay," said Annie. "We're already soaking wet anyway!"

With the rain pounding them, Jack and Annie started down 25th Street toward the Strand.

"The storm's getting bad!" shouted Annie.

"And it's going to get a lot worse!" said Jack.

The wind pushed them down the street to the waterfront.

Clam shacks, candy stores, and gift shops lined the boardwalk along the Strand. A crowd of sightseers, young and old, stood on the beach, cheering the huge waves.

The waves hit a long pier, and seawater shot into the air. The water splashed against the bathhouses on the pier, where swimmers changed their clothes in sunny weather.

Annie and Jack dashed across the Strand to the beach.

"Listen, everyone!" shouted Annie. "You're all in danger! A huge storm surge is coming! Leave the beach!"

"Run to high ground!" shouted Jack. "Now! *Now!*"

"Uptown!" yelled Annie. "Go uptown! Now!"

Jack and Annie both yelled as loudly as they

could. But no one seemed to hear them over the roar of the waves.

Jack moved closer to the crowd. "Listen! Listen, everyone!" he yelled. "A terrible storm is coming! The worst natural disaster in U.S. history!"

"Jack!" Annie screamed. "Jack, look! The storm surge!"

Jack turned around. Out at sea, the waves were gigantic! The storm surge had begun!

4

THE FLOOD

The giant waves slammed over the pier. They completely destroyed the bathhouses. Their broken wooden planks crashed into the sea.

The people on the beach screamed. They tried to flee from the incoming waves.

Jack and Annie ran with the crowd of people across the Strand to the boardwalk.

The surging waves rolled after them. Seawater swept over the beach and across the Strand. It covered the boardwalk and flooded the shops.

Jack and Annie began wading with the crowd

up 25th Street. The water was knee-deep and rising fast.

People rushed out of flooded stores and houses. They carried pets, children, and suitcases. They joined the others heading toward higher ground.

Jack saw a toddler slip from a man's shoulders
into the churning seawater.

Jack grabbed the boy and pulled him out of the
water.

"Thank you!" the boy's father cried. "Are you
alone? Do you need help?"

"No thanks!" shouted Jack.

"Buddy! Bailey!" a girl screamed. Her two
small dogs had slipped out of a basket.

Jack and Annie scooped up the dogs before the

water could sweep them away. They carried them back to the girl.

"Thank you!" she cried as they handed her the trembling dogs.

"Help!" someone yelled.

An old man was clinging to a lamppost, fighting the wind. Jack and Annie each put an arm around him. He pointed to a young woman, and Jack and Annie helped him wade through the water to her.

"Thank you!" the woman yelled. "Do you need help?"

"We're fine!" said Annie.

Jack and Annie forged on through the wind, rain, and rising seawater, helping anyone they could. Roof shingles and tiles flew off houses. Shutters flew off windows.

A fierce gust of wind knocked Jack and Annie over. They fell into the floodwater. They struggled to get back on their feet. They fell again. They got up again.

They used all their strength to keep moving. The street was like a river now. The seawater was above their waists—and still rising!

"Avenue L!" shouted Jack, pointing at a sign. "That's where the tree house is! It's a safe place to be for now."

"Okay!" said Annie. "We can climb up and figure out how to be more helpful."

As others kept moving up 25th Street, Jack and Annie turned onto Avenue L. The avenue was flooded now, too. They pushed past barrels, boards, and branches. Wreckage floated everywhere.

"There's the fence!" said Annie.

The top of the iron fence barely showed above the floodwater. The blue house was still standing. The tree house was still in the oak tree.

Jack and Annie hauled themselves over the iron fence and swam toward the oak. They grabbed low branches and clung to them. Jack looked around. The rope ladder was missing!

"It's up there!" said Annie.

The wind had blown the ladder over a branch. It was much too high to reach.

As Jack and Annie clung to the tree, lightning flashed in the sky. Thunder boomed.

More wreckage floated past—shingles, shutters, and fence posts. A big wooden door crashed into the tree trunk, barely missing Jack and Annie.

"We've got to get away from here!" yelled Jack. "Before we get hit by lightning! Or something crushes us!"

"Look! Someone's waving!" cried Annie. "From the porch of the blue house!"

A tall, thin woman was calling to them from her dry porch.

The woman held up a coil of rope. She beckoned

to Jack and Annie and shouted. Jack couldn't understand her words.

"She wants to help us!" said Annie. She waved back at the woman.

The woman threw the rope out to them. The end floated on the water near the oak tree.

Annie plunged into the floodwaters. Jack

followed. They both grabbed the rope. The water was up to their necks! They held the rope tightly to keep from being swept away by the current.

The woman on the porch pulled them toward the house. Hanging on to the rope, Jack and Annie slowly plowed through the water.

When they reached the steps, they dragged themselves up to the porch. The woman dropped the rope and opened her front door.

"Come in!" she cried. She pulled Jack and Annie into her house. Then she slammed the door against the storm.

5

ROSE AND LILY

Jack and Annie staggered into the house. They were both shaking. Their shoes and stockings were gone. Their wet clothes were torn.

"You poor children!" cried the woman. "I was waiting for my husband to arrive. I saw you clinging to that tree! Come sit in my parlor. Don't worry about the furniture. Rest! Dry out! You're safe now!"

"Thanks . . . thanks," stammered Annie.

"Yeah, thanks," breathed Jack. He and Annie followed the woman from the entrance into a lovely sitting room. They sat down on a sofa and tried to catch their breath.

"I'll get you some towels and blankets," the woman said.

As she hurried from the parlor, the wind howled and rattled the door. Rain pounded the windows.

Jack thought the hurricane sounded like a monster trying to break into the house. He remembered the giant waves attacking the pier, tearing apart the bathhouses.

"I still have our necklace," Annie said, panting.

"Good, good," said Jack. He had his knapsack, too. He looked inside. The Texas book was ruined.

Before he could tell Annie, the woman came back, carrying towels and two quilts. She handed the towels to them, and Jack dried his hands and face and hair. Then the woman wrapped one quilt around Jack and one around Annie.

"My name is Rose," the woman said, sitting down. "You must tell me who you are."

"I'm Annie, and he's my brother, Jack," said Annie. "We're visiting from Pennsylvania."

"We just escaped from the waterfront," said Jack.

"The waves got super high," said Annie.

"So where are your mother and father?" said Rose.

"They're—they're—" Jack didn't know what to say.

"They're at the Tremont House Hotel," Annie said quickly. "I know they're safe."

"Oh, but they must be so worried about you!" said Rose. "I wish they knew *you* were safe and sound with me."

A baby started crying upstairs.

"That's my daughter. I'll be right back," said Rose. She hurried up the stairs.

"Rose is so nice," Annie said. "And she's really strong—she pulled us both in."

"Right," said Jack. He was relieved to be in

39

Rose's nice house, but he was worried about the others still out in the storm.

"We have to help more people," he said.

"I know," said Annie. "We'll just rest here for a minute . . . and figure out what to do."

Rose came into the room with a baby in her arms.

"Lily, meet Jack and Annie!" she said. Lily looked like she was about a year old.

"Hi, Lily," said Jack and Annie together.

Lily stared at them with huge brown eyes. She had dark curly hair and rosy cheeks.

"She's so cute," said Annie.

"The howling wind scared her," said Rose as she sat down with the baby. "So, what did you see out there?"

"Huge waves," said Jack with a sigh. "They covered everything. The streets got flooded fast. Everyone was trying to escape."

"Oh, my," said Rose. "My husband, Lucas,

should never have gone to work this morning. I told him."

"Where does he work?" asked Annie.

"At a music store that's just off the boardwalk," said Rose. "I've been expecting him to arrive home any minute."

Rose stood up and walked to the window and looked out. "The water's getting higher," she murmured. "Lucas better hurry."

Jack felt bad for her. He remembered the waves destroying the boardwalk.

The wind shrieked. Thunder rumbled.

Lily let out a wail.

"There, there, baby, don't cry," said Rose, gently rocking Lily in her arms. "Think of this as a big adventure!"

A gust of wind shook the house. Lily kept crying.

"Hush, baby, hush. Papa will be home soon," said Rose. She started singing to Lily:

Hush, little baby, don't say a word.
Papa's going to buy you a mockingbird.
If that mockingbird don't sing,
Papa's going to buy you a diamond ring.

Lily stopped crying and looked at Rose. "Pa-pa . . . ," she whimpered.

"He's not here now, darling. But he'll be home soon," said Rose. She turned to Annie and Jack. "Lucas sings that song to her all the time. . . ." Rose looked out the window again. "He would do anything to keep Lily and me safe. I don't understand why he hasn't come home yet."

"What can we do for you?" asked Jack.

"You helped us," said Annie. "We'd like to help *you.*"

"Oh, you're both so kind and brave," said Rose. "You sound like true Texans." She took a deep breath. "I'm certain Lucas is fine. He's got to be fine!"

"I'm certain he's fine, too," said Annie.

Suddenly a huge blast of wind blew open the front door.

Jack and Annie leapt up from the sofa. They

rushed to the door and tried to push it closed. The wind pushed back.

Jack felt water wash over his bare feet. He looked down.

Seawater was streaming through the open door!

"Jack, look out!" yelled Annie.

The wind ripped the door off its hinges! Jack and Annie jumped out of the way as the door crashed to the floor. Seawater began pouring into the house!

6

ESCAPE

"Upstairs!" cried Rose. Holding Lily in her arms, she splashed across the parlor to the stairway. Jack grabbed his knapsack and hurried up the steps after Annie and Rose.

When they reached the second-floor hallway, Jack heard glass shatter below. He looked down the stairs. The first floor windows had broken. Water covered the parlor floor and was rising fast.

A chunk of the upstairs ceiling crashed to the floor of the hallway! It barely missed them.

"This way!" shouted Rose. "Be careful!"

Still carrying Lily, Rose led Jack and Annie into a dark bedroom. She shut the door. "There!" she said.

Shutting out the hurricane was impossible, though. The windows in the bedroom were broken. Glass was everywhere. Wind and rainwater swirled in. Jagged pieces of roof shingles blew inside.

"Get down! Cover your heads!" Rose cried.

Shielding Lily, Rose knelt between the wall and the bed. Jack and Annie crouched behind her. The baby buried her face against Rose.

The house swayed back and forth. Jack felt water under his feet. It was seeping under the bedroom door!

"We need to get higher!" said Rose. "The roof!"

"How?" said Jack.

"Follow me!" said Rose. Carrying Lily, she led Jack and Annie out of the bedroom.

The rising seawater had reached the upstairs

hall. Rain was pouring through a giant hole in the roof.

"If we can just get up there—on the roof—we can get above the water!" said Rose.

"We can climb on furniture!" said Annie.

"Good!" said Rose. "The dresser! The chest! The chair!"

Jack and Annie pushed a tall dresser under the hole in the ceiling. They hoisted a chair on top of the dresser. Then they pushed a blanket chest against the dresser to help them climb up.

"Rose, you go first!" said Jack. "Use the chest to get up onto the dresser. Then use the chair to get to the roof. Once you're safe, we'll hand Lily up."

Annie took the baby from Rose. She whispered softly to her as Rose climbed from the chest onto the top of the dresser.

"Careful!" said Jack.

Rose then climbed onto the chair. She grabbed

the edge of the torn roof and hauled herself up. "Now Lily!" she called to Jack and Annie.

Jack climbed up on the chest, then the dresser. Then he stood up on the chair and reached down as Annie held the baby up to him.

The baby was heavier than Jack had expected! He steadied himself on the chair, then lifted Lily up toward Rose.

Jack held the baby as high as he could. Rose grabbed Lily and pulled her onto the roof.

"You go next," Jack said to Annie. He stepped off the chair.

Annie climbed onto the dresser. Jack held the chair steady as she pulled herself up onto the roof.

Jack followed. He stood on the chair and peered above the roof. The wind and rain pounded him. He felt the chair shaking. The dresser shook, too. The whole house was shaking!

With no time to think, Jack gripped the edge of

the broken roof and pulled himself up. He joined the others on the windblown, soggy rooftop.

Battered by wind and rain, they all crouched around the baby. They held each other tightly.

The house shook beneath them.

"How can we get to high ground?" Jack shouted.

"I don't know!" said Rose.

Jack looked around. In the last light of early evening, all of Galveston seemed covered by water.

Suddenly there was a loud CRACK. The house was sliding off its pillars! It was splitting in two!

Rose cried out. Jack and Annie clung more tightly to her and Lily.

There were more loud cracking sounds. Half of the house crumbled into the churning seawater. The roof over the other half broke completely free of the house . . . with all of them on it!

"Hang on!" cried Annie.

Jack and Annie held on to Rose and Lily as the wind pushed the roof onto the floodwaters.

Lily let out a wail. Rose started singing. Her voice was surprisingly strong. Annie began singing along:

Hush, little baby, don't say a word.
Papa's going to buy you a mockingbird.

As their voices rose above the wind, Jack saw crumbling buildings. He saw people floating on mattresses, on boards, and even in washtubs.

Jack heard cries of "Help!" from survivors on rooftops. He saw others hanging on to tree limbs.

He wished he and Annie could help everyone. But there was no way to steer the roof raft. Every time the wind shifted, the direction of the waves shifted with it. The rooftop kept turning and moving with the storm waters.

Lily finally fell asleep. Rose and Annie stopped singing.

"Where are we?" asked Annie.

Rose looked around in the dim light. She gasped. "The Gulf! I think we're heading toward the Gulf," she cried.

"The *Gulf*?" said Jack. "You mean we might end up out in the ocean?"

"Oh, no!" said Annie.

But the wind shifted again. The water current changed. The roof spun around and began moving in another direction. Jack didn't know what to do, except hang on to the others.

"Are you both all right?" Rose asked.

"I'm good," said Jack.

"Me too," said Annie. "Are you okay, Rose?"

"I don't know," she said. "I can't figure out what to do."

"There's nothing we *can* do," said Annie. "We have to wait for it all to end."

"I think you're right, Annie," said Rose.

Adrift on the black floodwaters, the roof raft rose and fell with the waves. Storm wreckage

52

crashed against it. But the current kept pushing the raft through the wreckage.

Jack and Annie held on tightly to Rose, as she cradled the baby. Drifting through the storm, they all rocked back and forth together.

After a while, Jack gave in to his tiredness. His head nodded. His eyes started to close. . . .

7

A Safe Place

"Jack! Jack! Are you awake?" said Annie.

Jack blinked a few times. "What?" he asked groggily.

It was dark, and the night was still. The rain had stopped. The water was calm. Branches and boards gently bumped against the roof raft.

"Look at that castle!" said Annie.

"What castle?" said Rose.

"What castle?" echoed Jack. In a daze, he looked around at the darkness.

"Over there," said Annie.

A full moon peeked out from the clouds. Moonlight shone on castle towers rising above the water.

"Oh, man," said Jack. "Is that a real castle?"

"No, I'm afraid not," said Rose. "It's a school run by Catholic nuns. It's called the Ursuline Academy."

"Ursuline Academy?" said Jack. He sat straight up, fully awake.

"Ursuline Academy!" exclaimed Annie. "I don't believe it!"

"What? Why?" asked Rose.

"That's a safe place!" said Annie. "We read about it in our Texas book! People survived the hurricane there!"

"What are you talking about?" said Rose.

"Annie, you're remembering the description in our guidebook," Jack said quickly. "The book just said it was a 'tall, sturdy building'. You must have dreamed the rest."

"Oh, right," Annie said. "I dreamed it. But it definitely looks like a tall, sturdy place. Doesn't it?"

"It looks *dark*," said Rose.

"I know," said Annie. "But I'll bet lots of people are inside the Ursuline Academy. And I feel like they're safe."

"I'm feeling that, too," said Jack. "I think we should go there."

"But how do we get there?" said Rose.

"Jack and I can get in the water and push the roof," said Annie. "We're good swimmers."

"Oh, no, no. That's too dangerous," said Rose. "There's wreckage everywhere."

"Maybe we can use some of it," said Annie.

"What do you mean?" said Rose.

"We could try to find something to use as paddles," said Annie.

"Good idea," said Jack.

He and Annie leaned over the edge of the raft, searching the water.

Jack lifted up part of a chair. Annie retrieved a torn basket.

"These won't work," said Jack. They put them back into the water.

"Hey, *this* might," said Annie. She hauled a flat wooden fence picket onto the raft.

"Try it," said Jack.

Annie knelt on the roof. She pushed the narrow slat through the water.

The raft moved—but only a little.

"We need a second paddle," said Annie. "For the other side."

"Look, a broom," said Jack. He lifted a broomstick out of the water. A flat bundle of wet straw was tied tightly at the end.

Jack pushed the straw end of the broom through the water. At the same time, Annie pushed with her fence-paddle.

"We're moving!" said Rose.

Jack and Annie kept paddling the raft toward

the moonlit towers of the Ursuline Academy. As they drew closer, they saw that the massive building was partly damaged. Its tall, arched windows were smashed.

But suddenly a light appeared.

"Hello!" Rose shouted.

"Hello!" a woman called back.

"Is it safe inside?" Rose called. "I have children with me!"

"Yes! We can help!" the woman called.

Jack and Annie kept paddling their roof-raft through the water. When they got nearer to the academy, Jack could see two women at the window. Both were dressed in black robes with large white collars. Their heads were covered.

Jack realized that they must be Catholic nuns. The younger woman held a lantern. The older one was leaning out the window.

"Keep paddling! You're going to make it!" she called to them.

"Oh, my, that's Mother Mary Joseph!" said Rose.

"Who is she?" asked Annie.

"Mother Mary Joseph is in charge of the school and all the nuns. She is much loved in Galveston," said Rose.

The raft finally reached the window. Jack grabbed the windowsill to hold the floating roof steady. The younger nun held the lantern. Mother Mary Joseph helped Rose and Lily climb through the window.

"You go next," Jack said to Annie.

Annie crawled through the window. Then she grabbed the edge of the roof-raft. She held it steady while Jack climbed inside the building.

"We're safe!" said Annie.

Jack took a deep breath. They were in a long hallway with dark wooden walls.

"Welcome, all of you," said Mother Mary Joseph. "Sister Agnes will stay here with the lantern while I take you to the auditorium. But first you children must put shoes on your feet. Our hallway is littered with broken glass."

The nun reached into a bag and pulled out two pairs of shoes. They were both black lace-ups. Jack and Annie each took a pair and put them on. Jack's shoes were too long and too narrow. They looked silly on him.

Rose laughed. It was good to hear her laugh, Jack thought. He laughed with her.

"At least they'll protect your feet," Rose said.

"Come," said Mother Mary Joseph. As he walked down the hallway, every step in the tight shoes was painful for Jack.

Mother Mary Joseph led them into an auditorium. The huge room was filled with hundreds of people. Oil lamps cast shadows on men, women, and children. Everyone looked weary. Their clothes were torn and wet.

"Ohh . . . so many people," said Rose.

"Yes," said Sister Mary Joseph. "They're from every walk of life—rich, poor, black, white, young,

and old. Some have lost members of their families. Many have wounds or broken bones. All of them are refugees from the storm."

8

LIGHTING THE WAY

"Oh, my, you've saved them all?" said Rose.

"They saved themselves," said Mother Mary Joseph. "They all worked hard to make their way here. And they're still being brave and strong. Even some with injuries are trying to help others."

"Of course," said Rose, smiling. "Texans are at their best when things look the worst."

"That's true. Come with me," said Mother Mary Joseph. "I'll take you to the supplies in the front. We can find dry clothes for the baby there."

"Oh, thank you," Rose said. "And dry clothes for Jack and Annie, too, please."

"Oh, no, we're fine," said Jack.

"We want to help, too," Annie said to Mother Mary Joseph. "What can we do?"

The nun smiled. "Perhaps you could try cheering up some of the smaller children," she said. "They are all very frightened by the storm."

"Okay, we're pretty good at cheering people up," said Annie.

"Wonderful," said Mother Mary Joseph. Then she turned to Rose. "Come, dear. Let's find something dry for your beautiful child."

"Thank you," said Rose. Carrying Lily, she followed Mother Mary Joseph to the front of the auditorium.

"Where to?" Jack said to Annie.

"I guess we should just wander around and see who needs us," said Annie. She led the way down a crowded aisle to a far corner of the auditorium. There, some nuns were taking care of the injured.

A woman with her arm in a sling was trying to calm her fussy baby. Annie knelt beside her.

"Can I sing to your baby?" she asked the injured mother. "Maybe that will calm him down."

"Oh, yes, please," the woman said.

Annie picked up the baby and rocked him. She sang:

Hush, little baby, don't say a word.
Papa's going to buy you a mockingbird.

The baby smiled at her. Annie kept singing.

If that mockingbird don't sing,
Papa's going to buy you a diamond ring.

Jack heard a faint cry from nearby. *"Rose?"*

As Annie kept singing, Jack looked around at all the injured people. *Who said "Rose"?* he wondered.

The cry came again, louder than the first one. "Rose!"

Jack saw a young man lying on a blanket. His arms were bandaged. His leg was in a splint.

Jack's heart pounded. He hurried over to the man and knelt down. "Are you looking for Rose?" he asked.

"Rose—she's singing—Lily," the man said.

"Are you Lucas?" said Jack.

"Yes . . . ," the man said weakly.

"Oh, wow—hold on!" said Jack. "I'll be right back!"

Jack hurried to Annie. She had rocked the baby to sleep but was still singing softly.

"I found Rose's husband!" Jack said. "See the man over there with a hurt leg? He heard you singing that song. I heard him call 'Rose'!"

"Oh! Oh!" said Annie. "Get Rose! Bring her here!"

Jack hurried to the front of the auditorium. He found Rose with Lily and Mother Mary Joseph.

"Rose! We found Lucas!" Jack said.

"Ohh!" Rose cried out. She and Mother Mary Joseph followed Jack through the auditorium to the corner with all the wounded people.

Annie was sitting beside Lucas now. His eyes were closed.

"Lucas!" Clutching Lily, Rose fell to her knees. She touched the man's bruised face.

Lily started to cry.

Lucas opened his eyes. He smiled, and in a whispery voice, he sang:

Hush, little baby, don't say a word.
Papa's going to buy you a mockingbird.

Lily stopped crying. She reached out to Lucas. He took her tiny hand and kissed it.

"Pa-pa!" the baby said, and she laughed.

"Oh, Lucas!" said Rose. She was laughing and crying at the same time.

Lucas reached out to her. Rose took his hand and pressed it against her wet cheek. "I was so worried about you," she said.

"I'll be fine . . . ," said Lucas.

"Darling, our house is gone. We've lost everything," said Rose.

"No. We haven't," said Lucas. "We still have each other. . . . How did you get here?"

As Rose began telling Lucas about their journey, Mother Mary Joseph turned to Jack and Annie.

"Rose spoke of your great courage and kind hearts," she said. "I'm glad you found the way here. I fear few others will be able to find us in the dark."

"Why?" said Jack.

"They will have no light to lead them. We have very little oil left for our lamps," said the nun. "We must use what we have to light the auditorium."

Annie gasped. Softly, she recited:

For those in the dark,
Adrift and astray,
A single bright star
Can show them the way.

"Oh . . . oh!" said Jack. He'd forgotten all about their star necklace. He turned to Mother Mary Joseph. "Can you take us back to Sister Agnes?"

"If you like . . . ," she said, looking puzzled. She led Jack and Annie out of the auditorium and down the hall. Sister Agnes was still holding her lantern at the window. The flame was about to go out.

"We have something that might help," Annie said.

Annie took off the star necklace. She reached up and hooked the chain over the window frame.

The star dangled in the breeze coming from outside. Its tiny light was no more than the flame of a birthday candle.

"What a lovely thought," Mother Mary Joseph

71

said to Annie. "A lone star—just like our Texas star. Shall we go back to the others now?"

Sister Agnes gasped.

The light of the tiny lone star was glowing brighter—and brighter—and brighter—until the hallway was filled with golden light.

The light from the star shone through all the broken windows and out over the storm waters—*as far as the eye could see.*

9

IT'S GONE

"What a wonderful mystery," Mother Mary Joseph said softly. "Your light shines for all those who need us."

"Who are you?" Sister Agnes said in a hushed voice. "Angels?"

Annie laughed. "No, we're tourists," she said.

Faint voices came from across the dark waters. "Hello! Anyone there?"

"Yes!" Annie called back from the window. "This way!"

Jack and Annie worked with Sister Agnes and

Mother Mary Joseph for the rest of the night. They all helped storm refugees find their way to the Ursuline Academy. They called out again and again, urging them to come toward the light.

Jack and Annie helped people climb through the window. They led them to the auditorium. They gave them shoes and blankets. They were never too tired to lend a hand.

Just before dawn, the water started going down. By the first light of morning, Jack saw that the floodwaters had flowed back out to sea, like water draining from a bathtub.

The Great Galveston Hurricane was over.

Sunlight streamed in. Morgan's tiny star sparkled in the window. The glass star was just a glass star again. Annie took the necklace down and put it around her neck.

"Oh, no," said Jack, looking out the window.

Not one building was left standing between the academy and the waterfront. The ground was covered with pools of muddy brown water and mounds of trash.

Bells began to ring from the chapel.

"A new day is beginning," Mother Mary Joseph said.

"Yes," said Annie.

"Deadly storms are terrible," said Mother Mary Joseph. "But they always end. Then you start over. And you look at the world a little differently."

"Yes," said Jack. He was suddenly so tired he couldn't think straight.

"You both must lie down and rest now," said the nun. "You can sleep in my room."

"Thanks," said Annie. "But we have to find our parents right away, so they'll know we're safe. Please tell Rose, Lily, and Lucas good-bye for us."

"Of course," said the nun. "I will."

"And thank Rose for taking good care of us," said Jack. "Tell her not to worry—we know how to find our mom and dad."

"Are you certain you know where they are?" the nun asked.

"Yes. We just have to get back to Avenue L near 25th Street," said Annie.

"Is that far from here?" Jack asked Mother Mary Joseph.

"Oh, no, it's very close," she answered. "Only two blocks north."

"Thanks," said Annie.

Mother Mary Joseph looked worried. "Are you positive you can find your parents?" she asked.

"No question about it," Annie said.

"You'll come right back here if you don't find them," the nun said. "Promise?"

"Promise," said Jack and Annie together.

Mother Mary Joseph led Jack and Annie down the stairs to the first level of the building. All the windows were broken, and all the doors had been blown away. The storm water had drained out, leaving muddy puddles on the stone floor.

Mother Mary Joseph stopped in the open entranceway. "Thank you for all your help—and for your guiding light," she said.

"Thank *you* for helping *us,*" said Annie. "You remind me of a good friend of ours named Morgan."

"Me too," said Jack.

Mother Mary Joseph smiled. "Be careful, my friends." She bowed her head, and then left them.

"Mother Mary Joseph was the hero Morgan wanted us to learn from," said Annie.

"Right," said Jack. He quoted from Morgan's rhyme:

Learn from a hero
Who's humble and brave,
Who welcomes the hundreds
Arriving on waves.

"Look her up in our Texas book," said Annie.

"I'm afraid it's ruined," Jack said. He pulled off

his knapsack and took out the Texas book. It was soaking wet. All the pages were stuck together.

"Oh, too bad," said Annie.

Jack put the book back into his knapsack. "Let's go," he said. Then he and Annie headed out of the Ursuline Academy. They took each other's hands and began slogging through the mud.

As they walked up 25th Street, Jack looked straight ahead. He tried not to think about the destroyed city and the mounds of wreckage.

Instead, Jack kept his mind on home . . . on the Frog Creek woods and their house and their mom and dad. He thought of Morgan le Fay and Merlin and the magic tree house.

Soon Jack and Annie turned onto Avenue L. All the houses had been torn apart on that street, too. Only a few walls and chimneys remained.

"There's the iron fence!" said Annie.

They walked through the open gateway of the fence into the muddy yard.

Annie gasped. "It's gone!" she said.

"I know," said Jack. "We were there with Rose when her house was destroyed."

"No, not *Rose*'s house," said Annie. "*Our* house is gone." She pointed to the remains of an oak tree. "*That* was our tree."

The trunk was split in two. All the upper branches were gone.

And so was the magic tree house.

10

HURRICANE HEROES

Jack stared at the bare, broken tree. He couldn't believe it.

"It's gone?" he said in a whisper.

"Wait," said Annie. "Is that it?" She pointed to

a pile of muddy boards jammed against the iron fence.

"Maybe . . . ," said Jack. "What's left of it."

He and Annie stepped over to the ruins of the tree house. The floor was covered with brown mud. The roof was missing. Three of the four walls had caved in.

Jack started to lift one of the fallen walls.

"Hold on!" said Annie. She reached under the wall and pulled out their wet Pennsylvania book.

"Oh, no, it's ruined, too," said Jack.

"Wait," said Annie. She carefully peeled apart some pages. "Here's the photo of the Frog Creek woods!" She showed Jack the smeared page. "That's all we need! Get in the tree house."

"Are you crazy?" said Jack.

"Just get in," said Annie.

"There's no 'in' to get into, Annie," said Jack.

"Fine, then we'll just sit on the floor," said Annie.

Holding the book, Annie sat down on the muddy floor. Jack sat beside her. He'd gotten so used to being wet and grimy that he didn't even think about the mud.

Annie pointed at the smeared photo of Frog Creek.

"I wish we could go there," she said.

Nothing happened.

Jack put his head in his hands.

"I wish we could go there!" Annie shouted.

Jack felt the floor of the tree house start to move.

"Whoa!" he said. He couldn't believe it!

The wind started to blow.

The tree house started to spin.

It spun faster and faster.

Then everything was still.

Absolutely still.

Tap, tap, tap.

A breeze blew through the window of the tree house. Rain splashed softly against the oak leaves.

"We're home," Annie said.

Jack looked around.

As always, no time at all had passed in Frog Creek. Jack and Annie were wearing their own dry, comfortable clothes and shoes again. The canvas knapsack had changed into Jack's backpack.

The Pennsylvania book lay on the clean wooden floor. It was in perfect shape.

Best of all, the tree house had a window again! And four walls and a roof!

"I didn't know if the magic in the tree house could fix the tree house itself," whispered Jack.

"I was pretty sure it could," said Annie.

"Of course you were," said Jack, smiling. "Come on, let's hurry home."

"Wait, I want to look in the Texas book one more time," said Annie.

"It was ruined by water damage, remember?" said Jack.

"Yup," said Annie. "But I'll bet it's fine now."

Jack pulled their Texas book out of his backpack. The book was as good as new.

"Yay," Annie said.

"You were right," said Jack. He handed her the book.

Annie looked in the index. "Here!" she said.

She turned to the right page. "Oh, wow. Listen to this." She read aloud:

Mother Mary Joseph was an outstanding hero of the Great Galveston Hurricane of 1900. When the storm hit the island, she and her community of nuns saved the lives of more than a thousand storm refugees. Many people of Galveston called her—

Annie gasped and looked at Jack. "You won't believe this," she said.

"What?" he said.

"Listen." Annie read:

Many people of Galveston called her "a shining light."

"Oh, man," said Jack, smiling.

Annie turned the page and read more:

After the storm, 6,000 to 12,000 people were dead or missing, and 4,000 buildings were destroyed. But the survivors of the Great Galveston Hurricane did not give up. In spite of their suffering, they immediately began rebuilding their homes and their lives.

"Rose would say that's what Texans do," said Jack.

"She was so proud to live in Texas," said Annie. She kept reading:

Workers also built a high sea wall to help keep the sea from ever destroying Galveston again. Most amazing of all, they pumped sand from the floor of the Gulf to raise the level of the whole city. Today Galveston is one of the best-protected cities on the Gulf coast.

"That's really great," said Annie. She put the

book on the floor. "I'd like to go there again—in *our* time."

"Me too," said Jack.

"I'd like to meet the great-great-grandchildren of Rose and Lucas," said Annie.

"And Lily," said Jack.

Annie smiled. "But first, I'd like to go home and see Mom and Dad."

"Yup," said Jack. "I'd like that more than anything in the world."

Annie took off the star neck-  lace and set it on top of the Texas book. Jack pulled on his backpack and climbed down the rope ladder. Annie followed.

As they started through the woods, the rain gradually stopped falling. Streams of misty sunlight slanted through the trees.

Birds sang loudly.

"Remember what Mother Mary Joseph told

us," said Annie. "'Deadly storms are terrible, but they always end.'"

"'Then you start over,'" said Jack. "'And you look at the world a little differently.'"

"Yeah. Like ordinary things seem more special than before," said Annie.

"Like comfortable shoes," said Jack.

"Like birds," said Annie.

"Like sunlight," said Jack.

"Like family and friends," said Annie.

"Like family and friends," repeated Jack. "Let's hurry."

He and Annie took off running through the Frog Creek woods, heading for home.

Turn the page for a sneak peek at

Magic Tree House® Fact Tracker
Texas

Millions of years ago, amazing animals, including *T. rex*, lived in Texas. They existed before humans were on earth. Here are some you might not know about:

Deinonychus

(dy-NON-ih-kus) lived 110 million years ago. They hunted in packs and had a five-inch claw on their back feet that they probably used to kill prey or defend themselves. *Deinonychus* were about eleven feet long and had about seventy supersharp teeth!

Torosaurus

(TOR-uh-SAW-rus) had a skull over nine feet long, one of the largest skulls of any animal that has ever lived! *Torosaurus* were around twenty-four

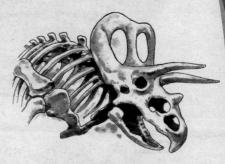

feet long and munched on leaves and other plants. They lived 66 million years ago.

Quetzalcoatlus

(KET-zul-koh-AHT-lus) were not dinosaurs. They were flying reptiles the size of a small airplane! *Quetzalcoatlus* had a huge wingspan that could reach thirty-six feet. Their beaks were up to eight feet long! Yikes!

Texas State Symbols

Mammal: Texas Longhorn

Bird: Northern Mockingbird

Flower: Bluebonnet

Dog: Blue Lacy

Horse: American Quarter Horse

Flag: Lone Star

Tree: Pecan

Hat: Cowboy

Insect: Monarch Butterfly

Reptile: Horned Lizard

Barbara Jordan
(1936–1996)

Barbara Jordan was a teacher, lawyer, and civil rights leader. Barbara was also the first African American woman in the Texas Senate. In fact, she was the first African American man or woman in the state senate since 1883! She then became the first woman from Texas and the first African American woman from the South to serve in the U.S. House of Representatives.

The Democratic Party asked Barbara to give the most important speech at the 1976 Democratic National Convention, when Democrats choose their candidate for president. Barbara was the first African American ever to have this honor. In 1994, Barbara was awarded the Presidential Medal of Freedom.

Red Adair
(1915-2004)

Red Adair was a legend in Texas. He was an expert at putting out oil well fires. It's one of the most dangerous jobs anywhere! Red invented a way to put explosives in the wells to stop them from burning. After that, firefighters must cover the well. While they're doing all of this, the well might explode at any time.

Over the years, Red and his crew put out over 2,000 oil fires both on land and on oil rigs in the sea. In the Sahara Desert, they once stopped a fire that had flames shooting 450 feet into the air! In 1991, when Red was seventy-five years old, he went to Kuwait to put out fires that Iraqi soldiers had set in a large oilfield.

He once said, "I've traveled all over the world, but I don't think there is any place better than Texas."

Six Flags

Six different flags have flown over Texas, one for each nation that ruled the state. Can you remember what they were?

In case you can't, they were: Spain, France, Mexico, the Republic of Texas, the Confederate States of America, and the United States of America.

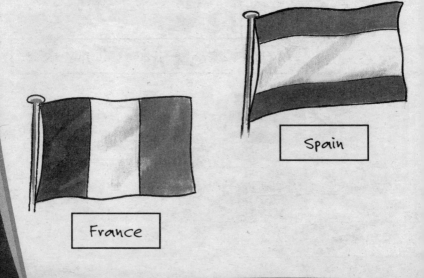

Spain

France

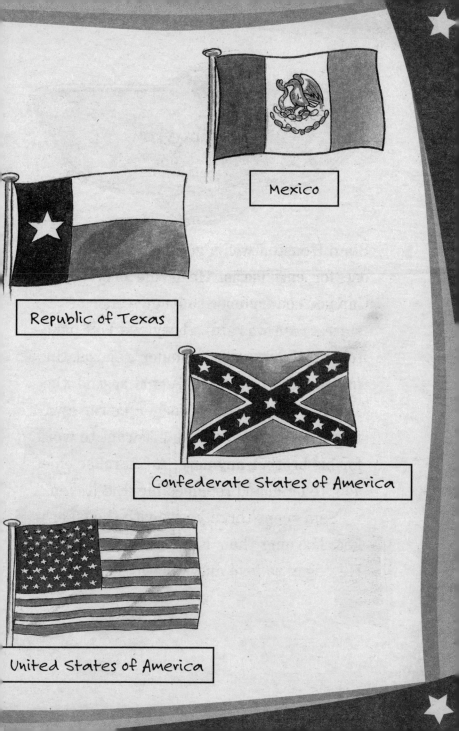

Mexico

Republic of Texas

Confederate States of America

United States of America

Sam Houston was a governor of both Tennessee and Texas. He is the only person in U.S. history ever to be governor of two states. Sam was also a lawyer, a U.S. senator, a congressman, a major general, and president of the Republic of Texas.

When Sam was a teenager, he ran away from home because he didn't want to work for his brother anymore. A Cherokee chief adopted him and renamed him the Raven.

Sam spent three years with the Cherokee, learning their language and customs. He began to love and respect them. When his life grew difficult, Sam often returned to be with the Cherokee.

Sam spoke out on the rights of the Cherokee. He once led a group of Cherokee to Washington, D.C., to meet with President Monroe. He arrived dressed in Cherokee clothing.

Selena Quintanilla Pérez
(1971–1995)

Selena is known as the Queen of Tejano Music. When she was very young, Selena began singing at her father's restaurant with his band. Her brother and sister were also in the band. Selena became so popular that when she was fifteen, she was voted the best Tejano female singer of the year. In 1994, she won a Grammy for best Mexican American album.

Selena played at concerts with as many as 60,000 people in the audience. Her albums have sold more than 60 million copies.

In 1995, Selena was twenty-three years

old. She was planning to fire a woman who worked for her. The woman shot and killed Selena.

Her fans were devastated. George W. Bush, who was the governor of Texas at the time, declared her birthday Selena Day in Texas. She is remembered as one of the most important Latin musicians of all time.

Here's a special preview of

Magic Tree House® #31

Warriors in Winter

Jack and Annie are about to meet
the fiercest warriors of all—the soldiers of
the ancient Roman legion!

Rider on a Black Horse

The air was cold and bright.

"Brrr, it feels like winter," said Annie.

"Yeah," said Jack, shivering. He could see his breath in the frosty air. "We're wearing Roman clothes. Too bad they're not warmer."

Jack and Annie both wore wool capes with tunics and boots. Instead of a backpack, Jack had a leather pouch attached to a belt. Annie had a belt and pouch, too.

"Hey, I'm dressed like a boy," she said. "This should be fun."

They looked out the window. Snow covered the ground.

Sunlight sparkled on a frozen river.

"That must be the Danube," said Jack.

An eagle cried out. Annie leaned out the window and looked to the right. "Our eagle!" she said. "And that must be our Roman camp!"

Jack leaned out the window, too. He saw the eagle gliding toward a cluster of buildings surrounded by a high wooden fence.

"Oh, man, it looks like my model," said Jack.

"Yep, and it's *dusted with snow*, just like in Morgan's rhyme," said Annie. "Let's go!"

Jack and Annie put their tablets and pens in their leather pouches. Jack dropped the coin into his pouch, too. Then they climbed down the rope ladder.

The sunlight on the snow was blindingly bright. But the air was bitter cold. Jack pulled his cape closer. The thick wool was warm and scratchy.

"Before we go any farther, maybe we should write something in our journals," he said.

"Good idea," said Annie.

They pulled out their writing tools.

"Watch," said Jack. He pressed the pointed reed into the wax and wrote a *W*.

"Got it," said Annie. "But we should write small so we can fit everything in."

Jack wrote *WINTER*. Then he looked at Annie, writing her own notes.

"What are *you* writing?" he asked.

"Rider on a black horse," she said.

"Where?" Jack said, looking around.

"Against the sun," said Annie.

Jack shielded his eyes and looked at the bright horizon.

A rider on a black horse was trotting over the frozen ground between the river and the camp. He wore a helmet and a red cape.

Oh, no! thought Jack. *Should we climb back into the tree house?*

"Hi!" Annie called, waving.

The rider raised his hand in greeting. He

trotted over to them. His face was mostly hidden by his helmet.

"Hail, children! Are you lost?" he asked.

Jack was relieved. The man's voice was friendly.

"Not lost," said Annie. "Actually, we want to visit that army camp."

"Have you family there?" asked the warrior.

"No, we just want to learn more about the Roman legion," said Jack.

"We're keeping journals," said Annie. She held up her tablet and stylus.

"Indeed?" said the man. "You are the first children I have met who keep journals."

"We plan to write what we see and what we feel," said Annie.

"Ah, young visiting scholars," said the rider. "Have you questions for me?"

"Um . . . yes," said Jack. "Why is the army camped here?"

"Legion Gemina Fourteen is camped on the

Danube to protect Rome's northern border," said the rider. "To keep invaders from crossing the river."

"Who are the invaders?" asked Annie.

"Anyone who wants to take away our freedom," said the rider, "and destroy the Roman way of life."

"Do you know how we can get inside the camp?" said Jack.

"Give the guard the password of the day," the rider said. *Mars the Victor.*"

"Like Mars the planet?" asked Annie.

"No, like Mars, the Roman god of war," Jack said.

"Oh. Who's the Roman god of peace?" asked Annie.

"Pax is the goddess of peace," said the rider. His horse pawed the ground.

"Pax. I like that," said Annie.

"Tell the guard you plan to report on the legion's hard work," said the rider. "Say you are visiting scholars under the command of the Imperial Guard."

"'Visiting scholars under the command of the Imperial Guard,'" Jack repeated slowly. "Got it." *That sounds really official,* he thought.

The rider squinted at the rising sun. "I must return to my station now," he said. "Farewell, friends!"

The rider turned his horse and galloped toward the camp. Jack and Annie watched him pass through the gateway.

"Let's go!" said Jack, and they started walking toward the gate.

"He was nice," said Annie. "Do you think he was an important officer in the legion?"

"No way," said Jack. "He was just an ordinary army guy. He didn't have a plume on his helmet. And he didn't wear armor covered with medals, like a centurion. Be glad he *wasn't* a centurion."

"Why? What's a centurion?" asked Annie.

"Super-strict commanders," said Jack. "They carry big sticks to whack their own men."

"That's mean," said Annie. "They should learn to use their words instead."

Jack laughed. "Try telling that to a centurion."

As they drew close to the camp, a guard stepped out of the gatehouse. He wore full battle armor. He carried a spear and a red shield.

"Hail!" said Annie.

"Word of the day?" the guard said in a deep voice.

"Mars the Victor!" Annie answered.

Jack cleared his throat and called out, "We are visiting scholars under the command of the Imperial Guard!"

"We have come to write about the camp," said Annie. She held up her tablet and stylus. "We

plan to spread the word about the legion's hard work!"

The watchman lowered his spear. "Welcome to Legion Gemina Fourteen," he said, "in the reign of Emperor Marcus Aurelius!"

"Thank you!" said Annie.

She and Jack walked proudly past the guard. They passed through the gateway and entered the Roman camp.

Magic Tree House®

#1: DINOSAURS BEFORE DARK
#2: THE KNIGHT AT DAWN
#3: MUMMIES IN THE MORNING
#4: PIRATES PAST NOON
#5: NIGHT OF THE NINJAS
#6: AFTERNOON ON THE AMAZON
#7: SUNSET OF THE SABERTOOTH
#8: MIDNIGHT ON THE MOON
#9: DOLPHINS AT DAYBREAK
#10: GHOST TOWN AT SUNDOWN
#11: LIONS AT LUNCHTIME
#12: POLAR BEARS PAST BEDTIME
#13: VACATION UNDER THE VOLCANO
#14: DAY OF THE DRAGON KING
#15: VIKING SHIPS AT SUNRISE
#16: HOUR OF THE OLYMPICS
#17: TONIGHT ON THE *TITANIC*
#18: BUFFALO BEFORE BREAKFAST
#19: TIGERS AT TWILIGHT
#20: DINGOES AT DINNERTIME
#21: CIVIL WAR ON SUNDAY
#22: REVOLUTIONARY WAR ON WEDNESDAY
#23: TWISTER ON TUESDAY
#24: EARTHQUAKE IN THE EARLY MORNING
#25: STAGE FRIGHT ON A SUMMER NIGHT
#26: GOOD MORNING, GORILLAS
#27: THANKSGIVING ON THURSDAY
#28: HIGH TIDE IN HAWAII
#29: A BIG DAY FOR BASEBALL
#30: HURRICANE HEROES IN TEXAS
#31: WARRIORS IN WINTER
#32: TO THE FUTURE, BEN FRANKLIN!
#33: NARWHAL ON A SUNNY NIGHT
#34: LATE LUNCH WITH LLAMAS

Magic Tree House®
Merlin Missions

#1: CHRISTMAS IN CAMELOT
#2: HAUNTED CASTLE ON HALLOWS EVE
#3: SUMMER OF THE SEA SERPENT
#4: WINTER OF THE ICE WIZARD
#5: CARNIVAL AT CANDLELIGHT
#6: SEASON OF THE SANDSTORMS
#7: NIGHT OF THE NEW MAGICIANS
#8: BLIZZARD OF THE BLUE MOON
#9: DRAGON OF THE RED DAWN
#10: MONDAY WITH A MAD GENIUS
#11: DARK DAY IN THE DEEP SEA
#12: EVE OF THE EMPEROR PENGUIN
#13: MOONLIGHT ON THE MAGIC FLUTE
#14: A GOOD NIGHT FOR GHOSTS
#15: LEPRECHAUN IN LATE WINTER
#16: A GHOST TALE FOR CHRISTMAS TIME
#17: A CRAZY DAY WITH COBRAS
#18: DOGS IN THE DEAD OF NIGHT
#19: ABE LINCOLN AT LAST!
#20: A PERFECT TIME FOR PANDAS
#21: STALLION BY STARLIGHT
#22: HURRY UP, HOUDINI!
#23: HIGH TIME FOR HEROES
#24: SOCCER ON SUNDAY
#25: SHADOW OF THE SHARK
#26: BALTO OF THE BLUE DAWN
#27: NIGHT OF THE NINTH DRAGON

Magic Tree House®
Super Edition

#1: World at War, 1944

Magic Tree House®
Fact Trackers

Dinosaurs

Knights and Castles

Mummies and Pyramids

Pirates

Rain Forests

Space

Titanic

Twisters and Other Terrible Storms

Dolphins and Sharks

Ancient Greece and the Olympics

American Revolution

Sabertooths and the Ice Age

Pilgrims

Ancient Rome and Pompeii

Tsunamis and Other Natural Disasters

Polar Bears and the Arctic

Sea Monsters

Penguins and Antarctica

Leonardo da Vinci

Ghosts

Leprechauns and Irish Folklore

Rags and Riches: Kids in the Time of Charles Dickens

Snakes and Other Reptiles

Dog Heroes

Abraham Lincoln

Pandas and Other Endangered Species

Horse Heroes

Heroes for All Times

Soccer

Ninjas and Samurai

China: Land of the Emperor's Great Wall

Sharks and Other Predators

Vikings

Dogsledding and Extreme Sports

Dragons and Mythical Creatures

World War II

Baseball

Wild West

Texas

Warriors

Benjamin Franklin

Narwhals and Other Whales

Llamas and the Andes

More Magic Tree House®

Games and Puzzles from the Tree House

Magic Tricks from the Tree House

My Magic Tree House Journal

Magic Tree House Survival Guide

Animal Games and Puzzles

Magic Tree House Incredible Fact Book